Beautiful Creations of Poetry

By

Laura Lavonne Spence

Page Intentionally left blank.

i

Acknowledgement

I first want to give a big shoutout to my great mother, Tonia, for always having belief in my potential and that possibilities can come true. Like a calling. I am thrilled to be able to express myself by making creative pieces of poetry to share with others in the world. Also, my gratitude goes out to the team of Amazon Experts for their service in helping me make this book come alive. They were so supportive in finding out how I wanted this book to be created, so thanks a lot! Lastly, shout out to my family members who I know have my back even though we are distanced everywhere; much love.

Dedication

"May these unique pieces of poetry on these pages of this book bring joy to your life and uplift your spirit."

Laura Spence

Author's Note

Hello, my name is ***Laura Spence***, and I am a college student at Chicago State University pursuing a bachelor's degree in elementary education. I, Laura, received an associate of arts degree from Kennedy-King College in the year 2022. This is my first book ever created. I enjoy spending time with my family, and I am grateful every morning for being alive and for opportunities for growth and new experiences.

Table of Contents

Beautiful Dreams

These dreams take root deep in my core,
Yet I shall seek a wellspring of strength.
A bounteous source of life's rich allure,
To the pathway that beckons my fire.

≈

My fate is ever so close at hand,
I sense its whisper drawing near.
So, I shall sprint through distances vast,
Like a swift vehicle racing the dawn.

≈

Oh, dreams, your essence resides within.
Oh, success, I know I can shape my fate.
Oh, self, triumph unfolds with steadfast toil.
Oh, dreams, shimmering like dawn's gentle glow.

≈

I can hear victory's sweet song unfold,
Like birds weaving tunes in warm summer's sight.
The Earth spins onward through endless time,
And our visions endure for eons untold.

≈

Oh, radiant you, strive to shine your brightest.
Oh, cherished self-crafted, exquisitely whole.
Oh, passion, this is merely the dawn of our quest.
Oh, generous heart, sorrow soars like an eagle high.

≈

f I stumble, grant me courage anew,
And if I falter, whisper, "You can."

Laura Lavonne Spence

You can be all that your heart dares to dream,
For it lies in the driven spirit within.

Free Form Poem

True Friends Never Depart

rue friends endure; their roots hold fast.
Through storms and trials, their shadows cast.
A patient ear, a steady hand,
Together strong, like grains of sand.

My dearest friend, my heart's valid key,
You guard my secrets; set me free.
A locket bound with time untold,
Its photo cradles tales of old.

Though years may stretch and worlds divide,
Our laughter flows, an endless tide.
When winds rise, when tempests start,
True friends, steadfast, shall never depart.

Sonnet Poem

Laura Lavonne Spence

Joyfulness

Joyfulness, Joyfulness, seen on a great piece of art.
It is special from the heart.
I needed it from the start.
Ever since, it felt like my world fell apart.

≈

Joyfulness, Joyfulness, seen in a great piece of art.
In a garden where laughter does bloom,
Joy dances away every gloom.

≈

Joyfulness, Joyfulness, seen in a great piece of art.
Like a wedding photo on a wall—boom!
It was just taken from the mall.

≈

Joyfulness, Joyfulness, seen in a great piece of art.

Short Limerick Poem

Hopes Lives Forever

In the quiet dawn, the world wakes.
The sun spills gold on waiting trees.
Hope dances lightly upon the leaves.
Each heartbeat sings of brighter days.

~

Clouds may gather, heavy with despair.
Storms vanish, revealing skies once clear.
Trust the steps; each one brings light.
A single seed becomes a mighty tree.

~

Dreams are rivers, carving unseen paths.
Courage sails us to peaceful shores.
Waves rise, yet we embrace their height.
Brave hearts find strength in the tide that restores.

~

Remember when stars hid from your view?
Darkness fades; its lessons shape us truly.
Even thorns speak of purpose in bloom.
Hope lives forever, through and through.

Sonnet Poem

Laura Lavonne Spence

Laura Loves September

In September, Laura finds cheer,
With leaves that turn gold, oh so dear.
The crisp air is bright; her heart feels so light,
As autumn's sweet song draws her near.

Short Limerick Poem

I Am Thankful enough

Each dawn breaks softly, a gentle hum.
Each breath reminds me of where I come from.
The earth is steady; it holds my feet.
Its whispers flow, a calm heartbeat.

~

The sky unrolls in boundless blue,
A silent song, both huge and true.
I count each moment, tightly spun—
The laughter, tears, and the battles won.

~

In twists of paths and shadows cast,
The lessons glow, their truths amassed.
Each trial bends but does not break;
It strengthens my grounded roots remake.

~

I'm thankful for the storm and calm,
For love's embrace, a healing balm.
Each heartbeat beats in steady tune,
A fleeting gift, life's fleeting moon.

Limerick Poem

Laura Lavonne Spence

For We Are the People

We gather, bloom, and rise as one.
Laughter echoes, a common song sung.
Hands unite like rivers meeting streams.
Flames of belonging warm the coldest dreams.

We are the givers, a steadfast tide.
No walls divide us, no fears reside.
Colors blend in the palette of skin.
Our blood hums the same truth within.

Through time, we learn what hearts can hold.
In pain, in joy, we are pure gold.
Lines blur where differences once stood.
Together, we redefine the greatest good.

Fingers clasp in a timeless, sacred play.
In circles around the fire, we stay.
Homes are built on trust, unmeasured.
Each soul is a gift deeply treasured.

This is the world we weave anew—
All as kin, with skies fresh and blue.

Free Verse Poem

My Uniqueness Comes From God Within

In every heart, a spark shines brightly,
A gift from God, pure delight.
Your worth is clear, like morning dew.
Embrace the light that lives in you.

≈

With every step, let courage grow.
Each trial faced will help you know
That in your soul, a song does play—
A melody to guide your way.

≈

So, when the road feels dark and long,
Remember, you are brave and strong.
Your uniqueness is a treasure,
A glimpse of love, a boundless measure.

≈

Stand tall and shine; let others see.
The beauty of your spirit is free within.

Sonnet Poem

Laura Lavonne Spence

A Mother's Love So Sweet

Her heart is wide, a boundless sea.
Her touch is warm; it shelters me.
Her voice—a song— it soothes the air.
Her strength is unseen, beyond compare.

She holds the stars within her gaze.
She lifts the dark; she lights my days.
Her love endures like ceaseless skies.
Her faith in me will never die.

Ballad Poem

Endless Peace

In lands where time forgets to tread,
Where stars lie soft on riverbed,
A hush unfolds, serene and wide—
No war to wage, no tears to hide.

The wind speaks only lullabies,
Its breath a balm beneath the skies.
No clocks, no rush, no need to race—
Just silence wrapped in nature's grace.

Mountains bow in quiet prayer,
Oceans dream without despair.
Each leaf, each stone, each drifting cloud
Wears peace like robes—unscarred, unbowed.

No borders drawn, no names to claim,
No fire, no fear, no thirst for fame.
Just hearts that beat in gentle rhyme,
And souls unchained by space or time.

So, let us walk this tranquil shore,
Where longing lives no more,
And rest within the boundless blue—
Where peace is all, and all is true.

Lyric Poem

A New Season of Strength

The leaves have turned, the air grown bold.
A whisper stirs in marbled gold—
Not of endings, but of birth,
A quiet quake beneath the earth.

⁓

The frost retreats, the roots awake.
The soul begins its slow remake.
No longer bowed by winds that bite,
It rises now in morning light.

⁓

This season wears no fragile thread;
It walks with fire where fear once spread.
Each scar, a map. Each tear, a seed.
Each fall, a lesson. Each wound, a need.

⁓

The sky no longer asks for flight;
It opens arms to grounded might.
And in the hush between each breath,
A strength is born that conquers death.

⁓

So, let the cold winds test your flame;
You are no longer just a name.
You are the storm, the calm, the song—
The season where the brave belong.

Lyric Poem

Breath of Life

Before the cry, before the name,
A hush arrived, without acclaim.
It stirred the dust; it kissed the flame—
The breath of life, both wild and tame.

It danced through lungs like morning light,
A rhythm born of day and night.
No trumpet blared, no banners flew—
Just air becoming something new.

It lifts the leaf; it bends the sea.
It hums in every memory.
From cradle sigh to final sleep,
It is the vow the cosmos keeps.

Invisible, yet deeply known,
It makes the flesh; it stirs the bone.
A gift not earned, a grace not sold—
The breath that warms the inner cold.

So, pause and feel its quiet art—
The pulse that paints within your heart.
For every breath, a chance to be—
Alive, aware, and truly free.

Lyric Poem

Laura Lavonne Spence

Blackness Is Something Special

Blackness is the echo of stars before light,
A canvas where galaxies learn to ignite.
It's velvet and thunder, it's rhythm and flame,
A legacy carved without needing acclaim.

It's the hush of the ancestors walking through time,
The pulse in the drum, the reason, the rhyme.
It's brilliance unbending; it's grace under fire,
A crown forged in struggle, a voice that climbs higher.

It's the curl of the hair, the sway of the stride,
The stories that live in the bones deep inside.
It's jazz in the chaos; it's gospel in pain,
It's joy that keeps dancing through sorrow and rain.

It's not just survivalist's style; it's soul.
It's rewriting history, taking control.
It's the light in the dark, the truth in the face,
It's power and poetry, rooted in grace.

So, speak it with pride; let the whole world know—
Blackness is special. It's fierce. It's aglow.
It's not just a color, a shade, or a skin—
It's the universe rising from deep, deep within.

Lyric Poem

Beautiful Creations of Poetry

You Will Prosper

Roots deep in still soil,
Sunlight finds the waiting bloom—
You rise, bold and whole.

Haiku Poem

Laura Lavonne Spence

Dancing With Praise

I lift my hands, the heavens sway,
My feet find rhythm, night turns day.
No stage, no script, no need to prove—
Just spirit rising in every move.

∼

The music calls; my soul replies,
A hallelujah through my thighs.
Each step a sermon, bold and true,
Each spin a whisper, "I see You."

∼

I dance through storms; I dance through fire.
My breath becomes a holy choir.
Chains fall off with every beat,
Grace flows wild beneath my feet.

∼

No silence here, no fear, no shame—
Just joy that dances in God's name.
The floor becomes a sacred space,
Where praise and power interlace.

∼

So, let me leap, let me be free;
This dance is how I come to be.
Not just a motion, but a flame—
A living shout that bears His name.

Lyric Poem

Pressing On

Winds push; roots hold fast—
Each step carves strength from the stone.
Still, I rise and walk.

Haiku Poem

Laura Lavonne Spence

Dreamer in the Soil

One seed, one touch of tender ground,
No trumpet call, no cheering sound.
Just hush and dark, a sacred start—
The soil cradles the dreamer's heart.

Haiku Poem

My Past is Far Behind

I walked through fire, through ash and rain,
Through echoes carved in silent pain.
But now the wind no longer moans—
I've traded ghosts for flesh and bones.

The road behind is cracked and worn,
A map of trials I've outgrown.
Its voices fade, its grip released—
I rise in peace; I rise in peace.

No longer bound by what once was,
I breathe in now; I move because
The past is far, a distant shore—
I sail toward strength, toward something more.

So, let the old tales lose their hold;
I wear new skin, I walk bold.
The sun is mine; the sky is wide—
My past is far, and I won't hide.

Lyric Poem

Laura Lavonne Spence

Still Be Healed

Even when the sky won't speak,
and silence settles on your cheek,
When prayers feel lost in drifting air—
Still, be healed. There's healing there.

Not every wound cries out in flame,
some mend beneath a whispered name.
The soul may tremble, soft and bare—
Still, be healed. There's healing there.

In stillness, roots begin to grow,
in shadowed soil, the light will flow.
Though nothing moves, though no one may care—
Still, be healed. There's healing there.

You are not broken, just becoming,
not undone but quietly humming.
The breath you take, the way you dare—
Still, be healed. There's healing there.

Lyric Poem

Knees Bent, Wings Spread

Fear stands tall, a shadowed wall,
but courage doesn't crawl.
It bends its knees, then takes the air—
a leap, a light, a dare.

Haiku Poem

Laura Lavonne Spence

Sisters Always Make Up

They fight like thunder, loud and wild,
then sulk in silence, each child.
A slammed door, a tear-stained face—
but love still lingers in that space.

One leaves a note, the other sighs,
they meet again with softened eyes.
A hug, a laugh, a shared old song—
they knew they'd not stay mad for long.

For bonds like theirs don't break, just bend,
and every storm will find its end.
Through every clash, they rise above—
sisters always make up with love.

Ballad Poem

Eternal Echoes

Soft murmurs of yesterday drift through my veins,
carrying laughter and sighs like forgotten songs.
Each memory—an ember glowing in dusk—
ignites the tapestry of who I've become.

Time's river may carry us beyond sight,
but love's current binds us through every tide.
In these reflections, our stories converge—
eternal echoes humming beneath the stars.

Lyric Poem

Laura Lavonne Spence

Dusk's Whisper

As twilight weaves its gentle hush across the sky,
I pause on the threshold between now and what's next.
Here, in the quiet, I feel the promise of morning—
a soft reminder that every ending births a fresh
beginning.

Lyric Quatrain

Flight of the Heart

Let these verses awaken your hidden song,
A steady thread of hope at the break of dawn.
Carry the warmth of laughter like a gentle light,
A quiet flame to guide you through the night.

The world awaits the colors only you can bring,
Each choice you make, brighter than you ever dreamed.
May friendship's roots hold you when storms arise,
And joy lift you on wings toward open skies.

Fly on dawn-warmed wings into what's to come,
For in your heart, new worlds begin to bloom.

Lyric Poem